I0744771

STAR CROSSED

HAREM STATION

A CRUX & CORLA PREQUEL

NEW YORK TIMES BESTSELLING AUTHOR, JA HUSS, WRITING AS

KC CROSS

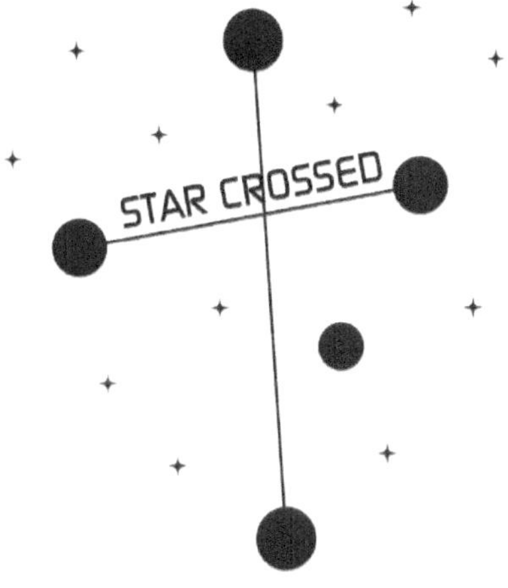

THE STORY OF CRUX & CORLA

BY *NEW YORK TIMES* BESTSELLING AUTHOR
JA HUSS WRITING AS KC CROSS

Copyright © 2019 by JA Huss & KC Cross
ISBN: 978-1-944475-85-7

No part of this book may be reproduced or resold in any form or by any electronic or mechanical means, including information storage and retrieval systems, without written permission from the author, except for the use of brief quotations in a book review.

This is a work of fiction. Names, characters, businesses, places, events and incidents are either the products of the authors' imaginations or used in a fictitious manner. Any resemblance to actual persons, living or dead, or actual events is purely coincidental.

Edited by RJ Locksley
Cover Design by JA Huss

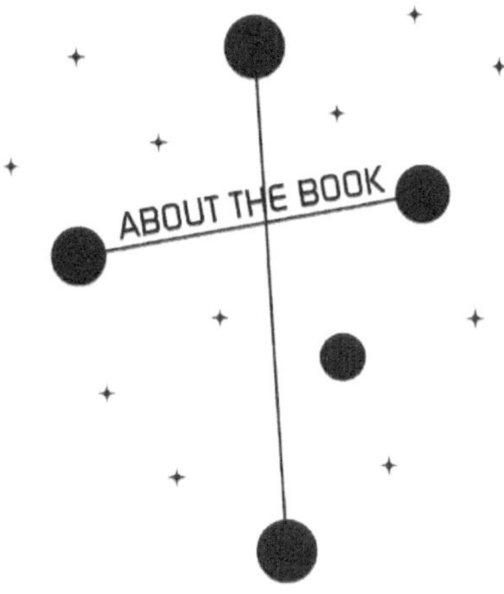

Twenty years before Serpint brought Queen Corla home to Harem Station she met Crux for the very first time. They were destined to be soul mates but could never be together. All they had was just ***one night.***

This is the story of Crux and Corla and how all the outlaw brothers came to reside on Harem Station. Meant to be read after Booty Hunter and before Big Dicker, it contains a star-crossed love story and secrets that are as deep and dark as space itself.

CHAPTER ONE

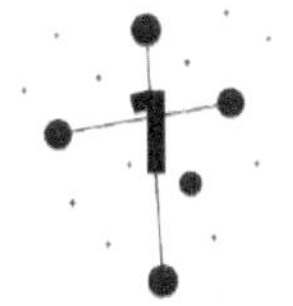

There are love stories and then there are star-crossed love stories.

Mine is the second variety.

When I met Princess Corla we were sixteen years old. I was still living in Akeela System. Still the son of the Wayward Station governor. Still had a future in politics.

She was the seventh daughter of the Cygnian king, destined to be his queen the day she turned twenty-three. So innocent.

But all that disappeared the moment she told me she was pregnant and convinced us to help her escape.

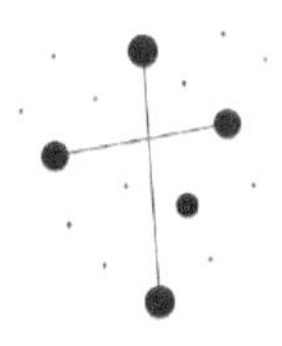

Twenty Years Ago

"Do you even know what you're doing?" I yell at Jimmy as I brace my hands on the two cockpit seats and lean over his shoulder.

The ALCOR gate is half a million klicks in front of us. Warnings are blaring on the comms system, telling us to turn back immediately or we will be annihilated into dust by more than a dozen SEAR cannons armed and locked on this piddly little piece-of-shit ship as we coast towards them on leftover velocity.

"Back the fuck off," Jimmy growls. "I said I got this and when I say I got this, I fucking got this. OK?"

"Akeelians are closing in," Valor says in the seat next to Jimmy, his voice squeaking a little. Then he yells, "They've locked on! Firing sequence imminent!"

"I'm sending the code to the ALCOR gate now," Tray says. "Hold for transmission."

"I'm arming the cannons, ready to fire back," Luck says behind me.

"A lot of fucking good that'll do," I mumble. "This piece-of-shit defense system won't save us."

"He's just working with what we have, asshole," Valor mumbles back, taking Luck's side.

Draden bumps into me, laughing and yelling as Serpint comes at him with a toy light sword.

"Got you!" Serpint yells. "You're dead! I got you!"

"You did not!" Draden screams back, grabbing on to my legs and hiding behind me.

"You're dead!" Serpint growls. "You died! I killed you! Go to regeneration for five minutes!"

"Would you two shut the fuck up!" I yell.

The whole ship goes silent. Well, as silent as a ship can when it's blaring emergency warnings at you. Draden looks up at me with those wide violet eyes of his and mumbles, "Sorry, Crux," as he and Serpint slink away.

"They're just fucking kids," Jimmy says, starting reverse thrusters to slow us down and give us a few more precious seconds to convince the ALCOR gate that we've got legitimate business.

"In case you didn't notice," I growl back, right in Jimmy's ear, "we're all fucking kids."

"Transmission sent," Tray says, his voice calm and steady.

"Cannons locked on the lead ship," Luck says, his voice the opposite of calm. "They fired! Firing back!"

We thrust forward towards the gate when the cannons fire, and Jimmy says, "Fucking hell! I'm trying to slow down, asshole! You know, trying to look like we're not gonna crash the ALCOR gate!"

"What the fuck do you want me to do?" Luck yells back. "They fired! I have to fire back, right, Crux?"

"Keep firing," I say, trying to remain calm. Maybe Tray should be in charge? He's the only one who isn't shitting his pants right now.

But the reason he's calm is because he's… not right. There's something not right about him. They did something to him last week. I'm not sure what. I'm not even sure I want to know.

"Ha!" Luck yells. "I did it!" Then he laughs. A manic, maniacal laugh. "They don't fucking call me Luck for nothing!"

The ship shudders and even more alarms start blaring.

"Oh, fuck!" Valor says. "We're hit!"

"What'd they get?" I ask, taking a deep breath.

"Cargo bay," Valor reports. "But it's mostly contained."

"Incoming transmission," Tray yells over the new, louder alarms. "Hold for screens."

"What part of it is not contained?" I yell, leaning down into Valor's shoulder so he can hear me.

"Life support," he yells back.

The screens come to life and a digital face appears. I've heard of this ALCOR thing. Some remnant, rogue AI left over from who the fuck knows when. And the reason I've heard of him is because he's been monopolizing the two gates leading in and out of his system for thousands of years.

Anyone who gets close is just… vaporized. Totally annihilated by the SEAR cannon weapon systems around the gates on both sides.

But Corla gave me a code. She pushed it into my hand just before I tucked her inside a cryopod and launched her into the Akeelian spin node, trying to get her away from her father before he took her back to Cygnus System to do terrible things with her.

And our baby, I remind myself.

"Where did you get this code?" the digital face on the screen asks us. The face is humanoid, but made up of numbers, symbols, and letters in the shape of a face. They fall down the screen like water.

"You're on," Tray says. I look up at the screen, the red light blinking to let me know the digital face can see me.

"Princess Corla of the Cygnian System," I yell over the blaring alarms. "We've got a message for the AI ALCOR but the Akeelians are firing and we've taken a hit. We need to get through your gate. *Now*."

"Please state the message," the code-face says.

"No!" I yell. "You let us through and we'll give you the message."

"That won't be possible."

"Then you know what?" Jimmy says, leaning his face up to the screen. "You can just fuck off, OK? We've got an important message from the future Cygnian Queen, motherfucker! You hear me? And if you want to survive what's coming, let us the fuck through! *Now*!"

"Shut the fuck up," I say, pushing him back into his seat with a strong grip on his shoulder.

"We're taking fire," I yell at the screen. "They're gonna take us out and—"

"Incoming!" Luck yells. "Incoming!"

"Last chance," I say to the screen. But really, I'm talking to us. This is it. We either get blown to bits in a matter of seconds or the universe saves us and we get through that gate.

There's a massive burst of light. So bright, the black-out screens activate on the windows. But this ship is truly a piece of shit. And it's not enough. Not nearly enough to block the light from the brightness of a SEAR cannon burst.

"I can't see!" Draden screams. "I can't see!"

"Don't look at the windows," Luck yells. "Don't look!"

And then… everything goes dark and silent.

The gravity drive fails, the alarms stop, the digital face on the screen disappears. I float upwards but my hands still have a death grip on Jimmy's and Valor's seats.

"I'm flying!" Serpint says, clearly excited about the lack of gravity.

"I can't see!" Draden whines. "I dropped my weapon and I'm floating!"

"You'll be OK," I call back to Draden. "Just hold on to something."

I should've had them buckled in. What the fuck is wrong with me? Who put me in charge? I can't even remember to put the damn kids in their safety harnesses.

Jimmy says, "What the fuck just happened?" in a voice that's now way too loud.

"That," Tray says, in his new, ever-calm tone, "was the Akeelians being turned to dust by the ALCOR defense system."

"We did it!" Luck laughs. "We did it!"

"Incoming click message from the ALCOR gate," Tray says. "Decoding now."

We wait in the darkness for what seems like eternity. Breathing in and out. Knowing every breath could be our last because life support took a hit.

This ship is dead. We are nothing but floating flotsam in the deep darkness of space.

"OK," Tray says. A shudder reverberates through the hull of the ship. "Light beam locked on. We're heading through the gate. We should reach ALCOR Station in six hours."

"Everyone hold their breath," Valor says. "If you think that's a joke, it's not. We've got seven people breathing air right now and it's not gonna be enough."

Somewhere behind me Draden or Serpint makes a big production of sucking in a deep breath and holding it.

I turn myself around, floating and feeling my way down the aisle to the airlock. "Come on, kids, it's time to put on suits."

The tell-tale sound of harnesses unclipping fills the ship as everyone floats up from their stations.

Because when I said kids, I meant all of us.

Because that's what we are.

Just a bunch of boys who got mixed up with the wrong runaway princess.

CHAPTER TWO

WAYWARD STATION

The first time I saw Princess Corla she was walking down the stairs of the Cygnian shuttle ship surrounded by an entourage of her six older sisters. She was dressed in a pink and silver ceremonial gown, denoting her as seventh daughter of the King and his future wife.

My father explained that to me on the walk over to the greeting hall.

"Wait," I said, as we walked through the door of the hall. "She has to marry her father?"

"Keep your voice down," he hissed back. "And smile, for fuck's sake. You're the son of the Wayward Station governor. Act like it."

"I am acting like it. I'm asking pertinent questions so I don't fuck up relations with the most aggressive system of people ever to live in this galaxy."

"Watch your mouth, Crux."

I huffed out a laugh. "Do as I say, not as I do. As usual."

"They are a genetically engineered species, as you well know. That question is unnecessary. Seventh generation removed. Use your brain, son."

I gave up at that point. Just looked at my feet, mostly. Ignoring the king and his daughter bride.

But that's the day I decided I was leaving this place. I didn't know how and I didn't know when, I just knew in my heart that this future my father had mapped for me was bullshit and I wasn't gonna waste my one life doing his bidding.

Little did I know…

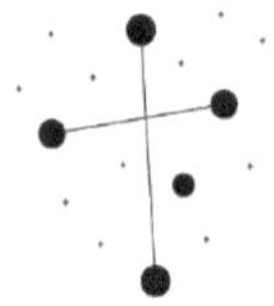

Right now it's the middle of the night and I'm in the governor's dining room getting drunk with Jimmy, whose father is the ambassador to Cygnus. Jimmy's pretty much my best friend by default because I have a very limited social circle here on the station. He's the only one my exact age, at least.

Valor and Luck are both a year younger. But we're talking an Akeelian year. And as far as maturity goes, it's more like three and half years for most other humanoid species. Luck's father runs security and Valor's father is the commanding general of six warships.

Then there's Tray, two years younger, and his father governs the AI who runs the station. He's a weird kid. And ever since he came out of cryogenetics last week, he's gotten even weirder.

The only other kids I'm allowed to associate with are Serpint and Draden. Both are twelve, which is super immature compared to sixteen. Their second cocks haven't even dropped yet. I have nothing in common with them at all. All they do is run around the station with toy guns, playing war games.

So… I'm stuck with Jimmy. Who, at this very moment, is going on and on about how he'd like to fuck the new queen-in-waiting.

"Please," I say, taking a sip of my whiskey. "She's got more guards than my father. You don't have a chance in hell."

"Did you see her hair?" Jimmy asks. "Don't you just want to run your fingers through it?"

"What?" I say, so annoyed by him. "No. It looks like strings of silver. And by that, I mean the actual fucking mineral. Who wants to fuck a girl with metal hair?"

"It's not metal," he says.

"How do you know?"

"I touched it," he says, smiling into his drink.

"You did not. You can't get within three meters of that girl."

He crosses his heart with a finger. "Swear to the sun, I did. She was walking past me and I just reached out and…" He sighs. "It felt nice. I'd like to pull it."

A laugh bursts out of my mouth, I can't help it. "Sick freak."

He shrugs, still smiling as he downs his drink. "You have your kinks, I have mine."

"Yeah, I know yours. They all involve sex bots on X Level."

"Don't knock it until you try it, Crux. Those sex bots know exactly what to do with two cocks."

"Sick. Freak. How do you even get down there? My father would fucking blow if he caught me with a sex bot."

"I have my ways."

"Seriously," I say. "How?"

He leans in, all secretive like, and whispers, "Tray. He hacked into the AI."

"He did not."

"Shhh," Jimmy says. "He did so. They leveled him up when they took him into cryogenetics. And I've got a good thing going with that little weirdo, so don't ruin it for me by blabbing your mouth off to your father."

"Like I even talk to my father." I huff, pouring myself another drink from the decanter the bartender left for us. "And what the fuck does that mean, anyway? Leveled him up?"

Jimmy opens his mouth to answer but before he can get any words out, the double doors leading into the dining room burst open and three Cygnian guards come through, looking around, subvocalizing security details.

"What the fuck?" Jimmy says. "Does the king need a midnight snack?"

But it's not the king who enters, it's Princess Corla. Silver hair shining in the overhead lights, wearing a pink dressing gown that looks too pretty to sleep in. Eyes darting straight to mine.

I squint at her.

"What's she doing here?" Jimmy asks.

"No clue," I say. "But I think this is our cue to leave."

"Leave me," the princess commands. Her guards make protests, but she holds up a hand. "I'm just getting tea." More whispered arguments from her security. "That one is the governor's son and the other one is the ambassador's son. What do you think they're going to do to me if I have a five-minute cup of tea alone?"

Jimmy snickers. Clearly he's got an idea.

"Enough," Corla snaps, when the guards continue. "You work for me and I just gave you an order. Either you follow it or I'll wake the king and get his opinion on the matter."

Everyone in the room, including Jimmy and me, just stares at the bossy girl with a mixture of shock and admiration.

They leave, closing the doors loudly as they go.

Princess Corla folds her hands in front of her, then smiles at us.

No. She smiles at me.

"Good evening, Crux," she says. "May I have a word with you?"

I glance at Jimmy, who lets out a laugh.

"Alone," she adds sharply.

"Hey," Jimmy says, holding up his hands. "I'm going." He sets his glass down, shoots me a wink, then whispers, "Go get her," as he straightens his high-necked collar and walks towards the door.

His fingertips brush through Corla's hair as he passes her, but before she can turn and shoot him a glare, he's got the doors open and he's stepping through into the waiting group of Cygnian security.

I raise my eyebrows at Corla as the doors slam closed again. "So… what can I do for you, princess?"

She looks over her shoulder, like she's nervous, then starts walking quickly towards me. "Touch me," she says.

"What?"

"Quick," she whispers. "Touch me. I need to know, because if it's true, it changes everything and I need to make new plans."

"What the hell are you talking about?"

"Don't you know why I'm here?"

"Uh… to foster better relations between the Cygnians and the Akeelians?" I ask, parroting something I heard my father say.

"Duh, no shit," she snaps. "I mean… you know, what they *expect* us to do."

"Ummm… what are you talking about? What do you mean, *us*?"

"Oh, for fuck's sake," she says, wiping her forehead with the back of her hand as she lets out a long sigh. "Can you just touch me? Please. Because… you're a myth, OK? A fantasy. Or… I don't know. A monster from a very dark fairy tale. I just need to know which. I need to know what's true and what's not, because I can't go through with this, Crux. It will be the end of everything if we do this."

"Do what?" I'm so confused right now. Because she seems to know who I am and the only thing I know about her is that she's gonna marry her father on her twenty-third birthday. And that's still gross, even if she is seven generations removed. "What the hell are you talking about?"

"You really don't know? Your father didn't tell you why I'm here? What you're expected to do?"

"Ahhh… uhhhh… be nice to you?" I offer, hopeful. Because I'm starting to get a very sick feeling in my stomach.

"No, you simpleton. I'm here—*we're* here," she amends—"to make a baby."

"What?" I laugh so loud she rushes forward in a panic and cups her hand over my mouth.

And in that instant—when she touches me, when her skin meets mine—my whole world explodes.

There's a great flash of bright white light. And some kind of electric shock runs down my spine, and the station shudders, and shakes, and then…

Both of my cocks are suddenly hard.

"Oh, shit," she says, pulling her hand away to cover her own mouth in surprise. "It's true! You're really him!"

"Who?" I ask. My body suddenly on fire. My hands reaching for her hips. Pressing myself forward into her.

She pushes me away, gasping. "No, not now. I have to go. But don't worry. I'll see you tomorrow at the breeding ceremony."

"What?"

But she's already rushing for the door.

"What did you just say?" I call after her.

But she's already got the doors open, already crashing into the waiting circle of guards, who surround her and whisk her off.

And then… she's gone.

Poof. As quick as she came.

"Breeding ceremony?" I call out. "What fucking breeding ceremony?"

CHAPTER THREE

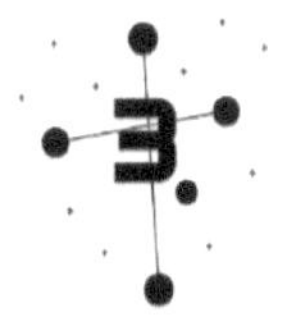

Waiting to be pulled through the ALCOR gate is agony. There is no light, there is no gravity, there are no screens to monitor, and the suits are way too big for Draden and Serpint, so they spend the entire time floating around the ship, flapping their sleeves and pant legs as they try to continue their game of war in zero G.

Draden can see again. At least well enough to play war with Serpint, so whatever. I'm sure this ALCOR place has some kind of medical facility to take care of any permanent damage.

Right now I only have room to worry about actual emergencies. Like getting through this fucking gate. I've only ever been through six gates in my life and all of them were at high speed. This slow, limping-your-way-through-time thing is unsettling. It feels like you're traveling fast, but part of your body is six feet *over there.*

Luck complains of a stomach ache the entire time. He's got himself strapped into a hammock off to my left. Tray is talking to himself in some secret language no one understands, still buckled in his station seat. Jimmy is sitting across from me, buckled into his stool, looking at him, then me, then back at Tray with an expression that says, *That dude should really be quarantined.* And Valor is holding on to grips by the airlock just looking out the window and repeating, "We're gonna die. We're all gonna die," over and over again until Jimmy finally threatens to rip his suit off and throw him out the airlock if he doesn't shut up.

I think about Corla, wondering if she got away, then decide she did, and that's why the Akeelians came after us. They need me to tell them where I sent her.

Then decide no, they're coming after us so they can drag me back to be killed by my father.

Then decide no again. She got caught somewhere on the other side of the node and they need me to make more babies with her, since the one she's carrying probably didn't survive her first trip.

There are about two dozen spin nodes in the galaxy and Wayward Station is in charge of the most active one. They are gates on steroids. If you were to stand in front of one you'd see a thousand gates lined up in the portal. It really is a thousand gates, but to your eyes it looks like you're looking into a mirror, looking into a mirror, looking into a mirror, that goes on for eternity.

They are used for stealth missions because they are untraceable. Once you go in, no one who comes after you can follow unless they not only have the same destination coordinates, but the same destination *time*. And even then, they'd still arrive far into their future.

Time is the tricky part because there's really no such thing as time. It's all local. It changes from place to place. Like, if it's eleven hundred hours here in this ship, and you wanted to know what someone was doing, right now, at eleven hundred hours on Wayward Station, it's not possible. It's unknowable. That question makes no sense the way the question, 'How bright is the sun in Akeelian City when it's night?' makes no sense.

The sun is as bright as it is. Period. Doesn't matter if it's day or night on a planet.

That eleven hundred hours and this eleven hundred hours have no connection. They are two separate times because they are separated by so much *space*.

And even if they did know the time Corla was aiming for, they could never get there. They could never meet up with her as she comes out of the node because their present on the near side of the node is Corla's past on the far side. And Corla's present on the far side of the node is their future on the near side.

Fucking shit hurts my head.

The point is, it seems pretty safe to shoot someone through a spin node. The odds of anyone catching you on the other side should be zero.

But everyone knows people use spin nodes to escape bad situations so that's where the bounty hunters wait. If you exit in a warship like the ones Valor's father commands, you're all good. No one fucks with you. But if you exit in a cryopod, like our silver girl back there, you're almost certainly fucked. The hunters pick up the pods as they exit, before the life support can unfreeze the occupants, and they hold them hostage.

And since it's the future, and text messages can be sent on neutrino waves that transcend space and time, it's technically possible that Corla has already exited the spin node, been picked up by bounty hunters, a message was sent back to Wayward—because that's where the pod is registered to. There was no time to secure an unregistered pod—and she could already be on her way *back* to Wayward through that same spin node as I sit here thinking about it.

My head really fucking hurts.

Suddenly we're going fast again and the sinking, left-behind feeling is gone.

The lights come on, the ship powers up, the screens all come back to life, and gravity returns.

Draden and Serpint crash to the floor with two loud thuds.

Mother of suns. Who the fuck put me in charge of these sun-fucked kids? I'm going to get them killed before we even arrive at ALCOR Station.

"Holy shit." Valor laughs as he stumbles over to the heap of suits containing Draden and Serpint. "Are you two OK?"

"You're dead, Draden!" Serpint screams. "Dead for sure now!"

"No, you're dead!" Draden yells back. "I shot you before the gravity turned back on!"

Valor shoots me a relieved look as Draden and Serpint both try to untangle their sleeves and pant legs from each other.

"Docking sequence initiated," Tray says. Like none of this commotion is even happening.

Everyone gets to their feet and goes back to work. Except Serpint and Draden, who just roll around on the floor insisting the other is dead.

"No one's fucking dead!"

It takes me a moment to realize I'm the one who just yelled that. Serpint and Draden both look up at me from the floor, blinking their eyes on the other side of their helmets.

"Sorry," I say. "But no one is fucking dead, OK? You're both still alive and that's how it's gonna stay. Now get your little asses up off the goddamned floor and shut the hell up!"

Jimmy glances over his shoulder at me.

But I just point my finger at him and say, "We're all fucking kids, OK? We're all just a bunch of kids!"

"Some of us," Tray says from his station behind me, "are more childish than others, apparently."

"Fuck you and your stupid leveled-up maturity." I still don't know what that means. I just know I don't like it. "I didn't ask to be in charge of this shit-show, OK? But I am. So everyone just… do their fucking job!"

I can feel every one of them side-eyeing me, but they don't say anything in response. Thank the fucking sun for small miracles.

"Now," I say, tugging on my suit like I need a moment to gather myself. "We're going to enter this station and do it just like we planned. Got it?"

"Yes, sir," Draden says.

There's a moment of silence and then we all laugh.

Fuck you, Draden, I want to say. But I don't.

Because Jimmy's right.

He's just a little fucking kid.

It takes almost an hour to actually dock with the station. But eventually the green light appears on the airlock, letting us know it's safe to open the door.

There's a long, narrow window in our airlock and we're all looking out of it when the door slides open. On the other side is just a small receiving bay, then another airlock. The readouts all say there's breathable atmosphere, but we keep our helmets on as we wait for the next door to open.

I'm carrying Serpint and Luck is carrying Draden, because there's no hope of them walking in their too-big suits.

The ALCOR airlock has no window, so we have no idea what waits for us on the other side.

And I don't care if I live to be five hundred—or hell, live a thousand different lifetimes—the one thing I never thought could be on the other side of that airlock when it opens is exactly what we see.

A sex bot.

"Welcome to ALCOR Station," she purrs, stretching out her hand towards Jimmy. "I'm Xyla."

Jimmy looks over his shoulder at me, grinning like an asshole who just accidentally found the Promised Land.

CHAPTER FOUR

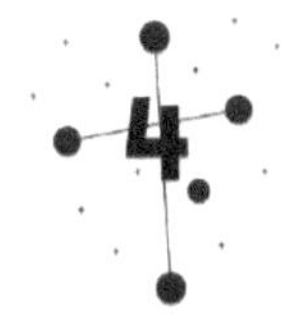

WAYWARD STATION

I didn't sleep at all that night.

I couldn't get her out of my mind. I couldn't get that feeling out of my mind.

What was that? That shudder, that chill, that light?

And a breeding ceremony?

"What do you mean?" Jimmy asks me the next morning at breakfast. We're in the same dining room. She was just over there. We were just over there.

"I mean… like… we're supposed to…" I nod my head a little and shrug my shoulders. "You know."

"Fuck?" Jimmy asks, squinting his eyes at me. "You and her?"

"Yeah. That's what she said. And when she touched me, Jimmy, when she touched me it was like… I don't know. Like the station was gonna explode or something. Did you feel it?"

"Feel what?"

"The shaking, you asshole. Aren't you listening to me?"

"I'm listening," Jimmy says. "It's just you're not making sense. Are you trying to tell me that the Cygnian king brought his daughter-wife all the way here to Wayward Station so the two of you could make babies?"

Then he bursts out laughing.

"Laugh all you want, that's what she said."

"OK," Jimmy says, putting up a hand. "What did your father say?"

"He didn't say anything. I didn't tell him. But there is a ceremony today at noon."

"Hmm." Jimmy huffs. "We're not invited."

"Of course you are. Your father's the fucking ambassador."

"I know, but… we're having lunch with some delegations from Cetus System. So unless your little mating ritual is supposed to be public, you're on your own."

"What am I supposed to do?"

"Do?" he says. "You fuck her, what else do you do? And"—he points his finger at me—"you enjoy it. Because you're never gonna get this chance again, mark my words. There are no Cygnian princesses in your future, brother."

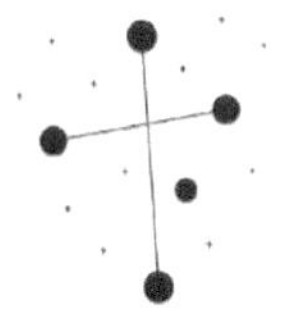

His father came looking for him after that and I was summoned by my father's security team to meet him in our apartments.

When I got there the place was crazy busy with people all coming and going and wearing special ceremonial costumes.

"Good," my father says. "You're here. Your suit is in your room. Get changed."

"Hey, uh… so what's going on today?"

My father, who usually turns his back on me when I have a question, stops and smiles. Puts a hand on my shoulder, squeezing it as he says, "Just a small welcoming ceremony for the Cygnians. Princess Corla will be there. I think the two of you will really hit it off. In fact, I've arranged for you to take her to the star bridge and show her around. Then have a nice private lunch in the park bubble. She's very nice. You'll love her, trust me. And you have all day, Crux. So just enjoy yourselves. You've earned it."

Trust me? I've earned it? It's not the fact that my father hasn't said this many words to me in my whole life that bothers me most. It's the way he says them. *Trust me. Earned it.* Smiling. Squeezing my shoulder.

"What the hell is going on?" I say.

My father looks around nervously, still smiling. It's only then that I realize not all these people are our people. Some of them are Cygnian people. "What do you mean?"

I decide there's no answers coming. Not from him and certainly not here, with them looking at us. So I say, "I better get dressed."

And I catch him glancing over at the Cygnians and nodding to them just before I turn away.

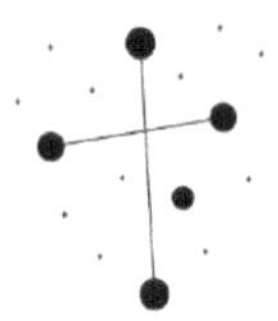

There's a suit inside a nyla-silk zippered casing hanging on a clothing tree in the middle of my closet. A tailor has followed me in, but he doesn't speak my language and I don't speak his. He unzips the casing and removes a ceremonial suit of red, and black, and gray.

"What's this?" I ask, pointing to the suit. Because I've never seen anything like it. Typically I wear a gray, bespoke business suit with skinny trousers, a hip-length jacket, and a shirt of contrasting color—typically light blue. On my feet I wear simple black shoes with soft soles. If it's a ceremonial occasion, such as today, I also carry a weapon and wear a black sash with white tassels.

This suit consists of tight black trousers and a black, double-breasted jacket with military buttons that look like ruby coins. The ceremonial ornaments are also unusual, a red sash with dark gray tassels, and off to the side are highly-polished, black, knee-high boots.

"Where did this even come from?" I ask.

The tailor blabbers and jabbers on about… something. Presumably the suit. And I realize there's not going to be any conversation. It's do-as-you're-told time.

I put it on with the tailor's help and he makes little adjustments with his fabric laser, tucking in the waist and giving me more room in the shoulders.

I stand, looking in the mirror. And then he comes at me with a… a *crown*.

"What the hell is that?" I ask, taking a few steps back.

Again, there's jabbering in another language.

"Can you get my father?" I ask.

"No," the little tailor man says. "You're late. Put it on." He has a very thick accent but his words are clear. "Face the mirror." Then he pulls out a rolling step stool and climbs up to position the crown on my head.

What the fuck is going on here? Since when does the governor's son wear a crown?

"There," the tailor says.

I stare at myself in the mirror, barely recognizing the eyes staring back.

And then I notice the people coming up behind me and turn.

"Sir Crux, this way, please. Everyone is waiting."

Sir? I wonder silently.

What the fuck is going on?

I'm led out of the apartments, flanked on each side by three unfamiliar soldiers, also wearing this new uniform, and up several levels to the ballroom. But they whisk me right past the large front entrance as more unfamiliar people whisper behind their hands.

We walk quickly down a long, side corridor and stop at a door.

It opens. A woman is there. Also weird. Because other than the sex bots on X level and the princess and her entourage of sisters, there are no women on Wayward Station.

"Oh," this woman coos. "You are quite spectacular. Come, everyone is waiting."

"Who are you again?"

She looks over her shoulder at me. Tight smile. No teeth. Then looks forward again without answering. We stop at a red and black curtain and she turns, pausing for a moment to suck in a breath of air like she's got a lot to say.

And she does. "I'm told you can follow instructions. Is that true?"

"Sure," I say.

"Good. On my signal, the curtain will open. Walk through. Enter the ballroom, stopping in the center. The princess is waiting for you. Bow. Not too low, not too high. Then take her hand. The music will begin and then you dance."

"Dance?" I say, as she raises one arm into the air.

"Now," she says, dropping her arm like she's starting a race.

"What the fuck is going on?"

She glares at me, then growls, "Follow. Instructions," between her clenched teeth.

I sigh and walk forward into the ballroom—which has been transformed into some kind of hellish black and red nightmare of floor-to-ceiling nyla-silk banners. There is an oval of people. On one side the Cygnians are all dressed in gold and white. On the other, the Akeelians are all dressed in black and red.

And standing in the center of the room is Princess Corla, frowning in her stunning silver and pink gown.

I walk forward, drawn to her. Eager to do my part and take her hand. Something comes over me, some kind of trance-like state and I get tunnel vision.

I don't remember bowing, but I must, because she bows back. And then I'm reaching for her, my fingertips pulsating with the anticipation of taking of her hand.

And when they touch the room lights up like the sun.

No. *She* lights up like the sun.

And my whole body responds with an electric shock that flows down into the floor and shakes the walls of the ballroom.

And then everyone begins to clap and cheer.

CHAPTER FIVE

After I introduce ourselves to the sex bot called Xyla, we take off our suits and hang them up in the lockers. My first impression of ALCOR Station is that it's dark. Also empty. Also silent, except for the constant hum of cleaning servos bustling along the floor.

"This place really is abandoned," I say, leading my troop of friends as I follow Xyla down a… walkway, I guess you'd call it. Only it's wide. Wide like thirty meters across. And it's just one level among hundreds of levels. It's sliced down the middle by an open-air space with some kind of clear plasti-glass acting as walls along the edge, and occasionally there are bridges leading across, or people mover-type things that crisscross up and down, leading to higher or lower levels.

But the people-movers don't move because… wait for it… there are no people.

Except us.

The floors are gleaming, even in the low light. Shiny, dark obsidian slabs. Where the hell did they get slabs of obsidian?

"It's not abandoned," the Xyla bot says. "We live here."

"You and… the AI, I presume?"

"And the bots."

"What bots?"

She stops and turns to look at me. She's pretty, of course. She was made to be pretty. Her hair is long and purple, her synthetic skin something between fair and tan. Her eyes are bright, bright lavender. And her body is… let's call it fantastically curvy. Huge tits, small waist, big hips, and legs that go on forever. She's wearing a pink t-shirt that's probably a size too small and black shorts that leave nothing to the imagination.

"What bots?" she asks me.

"That's what I said. What bots? There are more of you?"

She taps the toe of her stiletto heel on the obsidian floor and places a hand on her hip. "What do you call these?" She pans her hand over to a group of cleaning servos.

I raise one eyebrow at her, then look over my shoulder at Jimmy. He's paying no attention whatsoever to our conversation. He's just looking at this Xyla creature with lust. "Servos?" I say, answering her question.

"They are bots," she says, narrowing her eyes at me.

"Mmmm-hmmm," I say, pursing my lips and nodding my head. "They are. But…"

"But what?" she asks. I can tell I'm setting her off right now. Something about this conversation is really starting to rub her the wrong way.

I just don't really get that. So I forge ahead despite the inner warning bells. "They're servos. That's it. They barely qualify as bots, Xyla. They are programmed with a purpose and that's all they do. So I guess my question is... are there more bots like *you*?"

"Mmmm-hmmm," she says, mimicking me. "I suppose I'm nothing more than a servo too? I was programmed with a purpose. Should that be all I do as well?"

"Look," I say, holding up a hand. "I can see this issue is"—I channel my father, suddenly thankful I've been watching him placate aliens for the last sixteen years—"near and dear to your heart. I'm not trying to offend you and I'm not implying you have no"—for sun's sake—"*free will*. I'm just... doing my best here, Xyla. OK? I'm sixteen years old, I just shot a princess through a spin node, escaped an Akeelian warship, limped my way through a gate on a disabled ship, and now I'm here, on some abandoned station with no clue why I'm here, other than that princess I mentioned told me it was necessary. So," I say, letting out a long, tired breath, "I'm sure we have more in common than we don't, and I'm not looking to make an enemy right now, so can you please just take me to this ALCOR... *person*... so we can deliver our message and maybe these kids can be given a place to sleep and some food because it's been a long fucking day."

She smiles and says, "Very well. We can discuss this more another time."

"Thank you." I sigh.

She turns and we continue walking. She stops at the edge of the level, right up next to the plasti-glass half wall, and I realize there's a door there. She opens it and pans her hand to the open space just as a large, flat, circular lift-bot hovers up to the edge and stops.

The circumference of the lift-bot is large enough to fit a couple dozen people, so I wave everyone forward and then grab onto Serpint and Draden's hands before they can jump on, because I got these damn kids this far. I'm not gonna have one of them falling off the lift and dropping a hundred levels just when I think we're safe.

When we're all on board the lift hovers upward. Everyone is looking around. Trying to make sense of this place.

I've been to a few stations besides Wayward and this one is definitely unique. The open-air space is different, for one. All the other stations I've been on, including Wayward, have no open space. At least not one you can see from every level. There are always parks and shit like that. You need plant life on a station to create a viable biosphere, but they are mostly sequestered into greenhouses for life-support efficiency.

So this place is… nice. Feels more like a place you'd live. Not like a planet. I've been on a few of those too. And it's not that open. But there's a little bit of wind.

Still, it's dark, and silent, and empty. So it's super creepy too.

My only knowledge of this place was taught to me in school during seventh year. And it was only mentioned in the context of gate mapping. Because ALCOR Station has a monopoly on two gates. And there are thousands of gates in the galaxy, so you'd think that being unable to travel through two of them wouldn't be a huge deal. Except it is. Because this is the only route to get to the Seven Sisters.

Why people want to go there, I have no clue. If they told us that in class I don't remember. I just know that ALCOR's firm grip on these gates keeps people out of the Seven Sisters System.

This is a big deal in another context as well. A couple of explorers actually made contact with ALCOR several decades back. The story goes like this…

The team of explorers were granted access to the station, even lived on it for a few months, then they were sent back to where they came from.

Except they were… changed. They came back as cyborgs, and not the normal kind where people have implants or cybernetic arms and legs and shit like that. But the kind who had their brains and spinal cords removed and replaced with some kind of rogue hardware.

They went insane, tried to kill a bunch of people, then they were shot and dismembered for scientific research.

So yeah. Everyone has pretty much left ALCOR Station alone since then.

We ascend all the way to the top of the station and the lift actually becomes part of the floor when it settles to a stop.

Above us is an expansive viewing window and the stars shine down like twinkling beacons.

A hologram appears in the air. A digital man made up of cascading numbers, and letters, and symbols. He hovers for a moment, then descends until his computer-code feet appear to settle on the floor in front of us.

"ALCOR, I presume?" I say.

"The one and only," he says, panning his hands wide.

"Good. Well, we've got a message for you from the Cygnian princess Corla."

"Interesting," he says.

"How so?"

"Because I have no idea who this princess is."

I look over at Tray, who is staring at the AI in awe. Then at Jimmy, who is still looking at Xyla with lust. Then at Valor and Luck, who just shrug at me.

Draden and Serpint are tugging on my hands, chatting excitedly with each other about weapons they are planning to hunt down, and so…

Yeah. It's all on me, I guess.

"OK, well. Each of them has been programmed with a message. So if you'd like to hear them—"

"I would," the AI says, cutting me off. "I'm very intrigued."

Intrigued isn't necessarily a great response given this AI's history.

But whatever. We're here. And we've got nowhere else to go, so I bend down and grab Draden by the shoulders so he's facing me. "Hey," I say.

"Hey, Crux," Draden says, oblivious to the seriousness of this situation.

"Remember when the princess accessed your internal comm and gave you a message?"

He nods at me.

"OK, well, it's time to release it. Can you do that for me?"

He nods again, then taps his ear and spits out a garbled mess of incoherent words.

I look at the AI for a response, and find him frowning. "What's the next one?" he asks.

I point to Serpint, and thank the sun for small favors, Serpint has caught on to what's expected.

Because he taps his comm and spits out his message too.

Again, I look to the AI for some kind of reaction. "Keep going, please," he says.

We go in turn like that. Tray goes next, then Luck, then Valor, then Jimmy. And then the AI looks at me and says, "You don't have one, do you?"

I shake my head. Because I don't. "Princess Corla only said I was to deliver them to you."

I pause. ALCOR pauses. Everyone pauses, even Draden and Serpint.

"Well?" I say. "What the fuck does it mean?"

"I'm not sure yet. But thank you for bringing it to my attention."

"That's it?" I say. "We don't even get to know why the fuck we just risked our lives and the entire Akeelian Navy is after us now? I left my home for this. I'm the fucking Wayward Station governor's son. I think you owe us an explanation."

"I'm afraid I don't have one," ALCOR says. "But I do have an offer for you."

"Offer?" I huff. "Yeah, what's that?"

"Get me online. Give me access to the galactic net. If you can do that, you can stay and I'll take care of you. No one can harm you here. No one can get through my gates without permission. We will be a team."

I side-eye the code man, not sure what to say.

But Tray says, "I can get you online."

"Can you?" ALCOR asks.

Tray nods. "Just give me access to your core and one of those SEAR cannons I saw outside and we can thread a quantum neutrino stream through your gates. Once it gets to the other side it'll keep going forever. If we shoot them out in every possible direction and create a sort of geodesic vector field that can ride along the nodes and links in time and space, then—"

"Ahhh," ALCOR says with a chuckle. "Differential geometry. Such an ancient concept, I'd forgotten about it. You are a clever little monkey, my new friend."

"How the fuck do you know that?" I ask Tray.

Tray looks at me and shrugs. "I dunno, really. I don't even understand what I'm saying. I just know it's the answer."

I glance at Jimmy, who's got one eyebrow raised.

Leveled up, indeed.

CHAPTER SIX

WAYWARD STATION

We dance, the princess and I.

Just the way that woman behind the curtain told us to.

And everyone keeps clapping. They don't stop. Corla is glowing bright white light. Some of it leaks on to me and I can feel it. It's warm, and soft, and makes me want to... do things to her.

"You don't know," Corla says, leaning into my neck to whisper. "Do you?"

The only thing I know is that both my cocks are hard when they're not supposed to be. Every fiber of my being urges me to put them inside her.

"I need you," I say, my voice desperate and unfamiliar.

"It's OK," she says. "I figured it out last night after we met."

"I need you now," I say.

"I know. Just... finish the dance and then they'll let us leave."

I press my lips up to her neck and she glows a little brighter when I begin to kiss her. The clapping becomes louder for a moment. Like I just did something these people approve of. "They're not gonna let us leave," I say, almost unable to control myself.

"Believe me," Corla says. "They will. That's the whole point of this."

My mind is spinning with the implications of her words. But I can't concentrate. I can't focus. I'm not sure I even exist right now. I am nothing but urges and needs. All I want to do is fuck her.

The music stops and Corla stops dancing. It takes me a moment to catch up with what's happening, but eventually I force myself to look over at my father.

He's smiling so big. So wide. And my eyes are so hooded and heavy with lust and desire, they're barely open.

She's gotten me drunk. Drunk on her scent, and her light, and her touch, and there's nothing I can do or think about that isn't about her. About how I want to open her legs and fill her up.

My father is talking, then the king is responding. And then there's more clapping as Corla and I continue to spin—standing still in the center of the ballroom.

I glance around the room, find the woman behind the curtain beckoning me towards her. Corla has a hold of my hand, so when I begin walking towards the woman, I pull the princess along with me.

What the fuck is happening? I feel like I've lost control of myself. Like someone drugged me.

When I reach the woman she points to the curtain again and I move towards it on autopilot.

The clapping in the ballroom turns into a resounding roar as people cheer and yell.

"Just keep walking," Corla says. "I promise, it'll be OK. I have a plan."

A plan? I have a plan too. A plan to fuck her right in this hallway.

"Where are we?" I ask, suddenly becoming more aware of my surroundings.

I've lived on this station my whole life. Know it backwards and forwards, but I have no idea where I am.

"Something called a star bridge?" Corla says. "We can do it here if you can't wait any longer. Then you'll feel better, I promise."

"Do what?" I say, backing her up against the station window. We are in the star walk. I've been here before, my drunk mind is just slow at processing. It's a long tube of transparent plasti-glass and all around us the stars twinkle in the deep dark.

Corla has her hands on my shoulders and her touch—for the love of suns—her touch is so intoxicating.

"What's happening to me?" I ask.

"Just… here," she says, taking my hand and lowering it down to her belly. "Let me help you."

Her dress parts between her legs, the thick, woven fabric embroidered with silver thread opening for me as I reach inside. And then my fingers find her warm skin. She has no panties on. Just bare for me.

Lust fills my head. Some kind of animal instinct takes over. Her fingers are fumbling with the button of my trousers, desperate to get them open. Then my cocks—hard and throbbing, almost aching to be inside her—are in her warm hand. She pumps them a few times but that's all I can take. I lean into her, reaching under her ass to lift her up.

She opens her dress to give me access and then, without thinking, or planning—I'm inside her. All of me. Both cocks, thrusting deep inside her.

She gasps, and moans, and cries out like it hurts.

And even though I understand that I should care that I'm hurting her, I do not care.

I just… fuck her. I fuck her hard. Pressed up against the endless dark night and the bits of shining stars.

Something is humming in my ear. No. Some thing. A drone, I realize. A small, bird-like drone with wings that beat a million times a second.

I swat it away and keep going, her light becoming brighter and brighter as she moans and then wraps her legs around my waist.

And then, just when I think I will die because she feels too good, too perfect, too… everything…

We explode.

Light bursts up and out. The whole star walk brightens in a flash and the deep dark outside disappears, taking the stars away with it.

I lean into her neck. Unable to comprehend what just happened. Unable to move, or talk, or think. But my cocks have other ideas. They don't soften. In fact, they become even harder inside her.

"What the fuck?" I whisper.

"Twice," Corla says, glowing white light flowing out of her body. "We have to do it twice."

"I don't think I can—" But I'm already doing it. Already fucking her again before I can finish my sentence. My hips eager and thrusting. Her mouth making the most delicious sounds. So ready to come again, I feel like an animal running on instinct alone.

"Now," she says. "Right now!"

This time it's not a decision. It's a primal impulse. We come together once more. Moaning and writhing up against the side of the station.

We stay like that as her light dissipates, then subsides altogether. My mind begins to focus again. Reality comes forward, tapping me on the shoulder. Letting me know it's over.

The drone is still buzzing about. Corla is shuddering and weak in my arms as I hold her up and then…

We collapse to the floor in a heap and just lie there.

The tiny drone hovers in front of me for a moment. I lift my had to swat it again, but it just darts away and disappears down the tube.

"Holy shit," Corla says.

I laugh, then say, "Holy shit is right. What the fuck was that? I'm sorry. I'm so fucking sorry. Something came over me. I was… drunk or something. I don't know. I can't even remember how we got here."

"It's OK," she says, patting my chest. Her face is buried in my neck. And when I glance down, her eyes are closed. "You can't help it. We can't help it, Crux. They made us this way."

"What?"

She makes an effort to sit up a little and open her eyes. They're silver. Still glowing. She's beautiful, I realize. Her hair—God, Jimmy was right. Because I pick a few strands of it up and in my hand, unable to hold in the urge to run my fingers through it. It's soft, and sparkling with her white light.

"They made me for you," she whispers. "And they made you for me. That's all."

"What do you mean?" I whisper back.

She sighs, then pulls herself together and gets to her feet, holding out a hand to me.

I take it and let her pull me up, thinking I probably should've been the one to help her up, but… fuck it. I don't understand what's happening to me.

"I can't believe they didn't tell you anything."

"Tell me what?" I ask, tucking my cocks back into my pants and straightening my clothes.

Her dress is perfect. Like this never happened. I realize there's a hidden slit up the middle, covered by panels that flow over her hips. I realize her dress was made so I could fuck her in it.

"About the breeding ceremony," she says. Then she takes my hand and starts pulling me down the tunnel of stars. "Come on, they won't follow us. They got what they wanted and now we have one night to make our plan."

"What plan?" I ask, allowing myself to be tugged along.

She glances over her shoulder and smiles. "Our escape, of course."

CHAPTER SEVEN

"*Happy birthday, you little shit,*" Jimmy says to Draden as he ruffles his hair.

Draden is tall now. The years we've been here on ALCOR Station have been good to him. We have more food to eat than we ever did on Wayward. We have clean air, and a constant supply of water. Serpint, too, has grown big and strong. Over two meters tall, like the rest of us.

But it feels good to know they had a real childhood. That none of my friends will ever have to go through what I did with Corla.

I'm twenty now. Which means only a few more years before I'm considered a man. Akeelians age differently than other humanoid species, taking almost twenty-six years to reach full maturity. There's this weird in-between stage—the age Draden and Serpint were when we got here— where you're still a child in your mind even though your body is growing. It lasts until about age fifteen. Then you get muscles, and your second cock drops, and urges begin to take over.

Except there's no one here but us still, and it's becoming more and more difficult to keep everyone happy. Jimmy is the only one sorta satisfied, and that's because he and Xyla hit it off early. But they don't... do that. They are just friends. It's not enough for him. It's not even enough for her. Or us.

We all want to leave. We all want to find girls, and go drinking, and have fun.

In other words, we all want to *live*. Not just exist.

ALCOR has called a meeting today in the common room where we sleep and hang out. It's like a pod, I guess. Everyone has their own private quarters around the perimeter of the circular room. There's a kitchen, and some screens, and we have access to the net. Which satisfies our need for porn.

And Tray has been working on the virtual-reality sector—which he calls the Pleasure Prison—so we have that. He's made some cool places in there—a whole other galaxy, actually. Suns with systems and habitable planets. Ships that can travel faster than light. Cities and small towns on the planets. And no money required to do whatever you want. There's also people. Millions of fake people.

But still. It's not the same. It's not... *real.*

Something's gotta give.

We can't stay here like this. ALCOR Station might be our home, but it's also a prison.

"I don't know what to do," Xyla says, pulling me out of my introspection.

"Just replace it all," Jimmy says. "And get armor instead."

"What are you guys talking about?" I ask.

"Xyla. She doesn't want to look like a sex bot anymore."

"That's not what I said. I don't want to change me, just change the way people perceive me. So they don't think I'm just here for sex."

"We don't think you're here for sex, Xyla." I laugh a little. Because... no. She's like a sister to us, not a sex bot.

"Not you," she says. "The others."

"What others?" everyone but Jimmy, Tray, and Xyla says. And you can't miss the eagerness and excitement in our voices.

"That's why we're here," ALCOR says, morphing into a hologram in the center of the room. "I've decided we're ready."

"Ready for what?" Luck asks.

ALCOR spreads his arms wide. "For all of it. We need people. Real people. I've had bots working on building you ships."

"Ships!" Serpint says. "Fuck, yeah!"

"And I've developed an advertising campaign for the net. We're going to change our name."

"To what?" I ask.

"Harem Station." ALCOR beams in the center of the room like this is the most brilliant name ever.

"Why?" I ask. "That implies we have girls here, and clearly we do not."

"But we will," ALCOR says. "We will have lots of girls. That," he says, pointing to Draden and Serpint, "is your new job. You are now official bounty hunters for the new Harem Station."

"Oh, hell, yeah," Draden says, doing a little dance. "We're gonna go and get some girls."

"You mean steal them?" I ask.

ALCOR smiles at me. "Not steal. Convince. That's all. Convince them to join us. We're going to need a lot of girls, because boys, I have a vision for the future. We're going to turn Harem Station into the preeminent place for outlaw fun. I want the desperate, the jaded, the lost, the ruthless. I want pirates, and assassins, and bounty hunters, and soldiers. I want all the people this galaxy rejects. I want the Prime Navy—"

"Who?" Valor asks. "Who the fuck is the Prime Navy?"

"Oh," ALCOR says. "I forgot. I didn't share that with you."

"Share what?" I ask. I never know if this AI truly cares about us, is just using us, or is prepping us for some bigger, unknown part in some diabolical plan. But he's always made me nervous. I'm not sure how to trust an immortal self-contained entity like ALCOR. He's manipulative, and secretive, and when he says he has a vision for the future, he's not talking about a ten-year plan. He's talking about a ten-*thousand*-year plan.

I'm just not sure I can wrap my head around that.

"The Prime Navy formed after word got out that you boys were staying here with me," ALCOR continues. "It was an overreaction when I had to take out a fleet of Cygnian and Akeelian warships about a year after your arrival."

"What?" Jimmy laughs.

"It's not funny," I say. "What the fuck, ALCOR? Why didn't you tell us this?"

"Because," Tray says, "you would've had a problem killing half a million people just to make the point that you could."

"Shit," Draden says.

I glare at ALCOR. He smiles at me. He's no longer just code in the shape of a man. He's got a face now. Kinda nice-looking, actually. Young, but not as young as us. Light hair, blue eyes, and sometimes he has a shadow on his jaw like he forgot to shave.

I think this was Tray. I think all the changes in ALCOR over the years have been Tray and it kinda freaks me out that I have no idea who that guy is anymore.

"Anyway," ALCOR says. "The point is, the Prime Navy now exists under the false presumption that I can be contained."

"Hmm," I say.

"Don't worry, Crux," ALCOR says. "I'm going to make a promise to you now."

"What kind of promise?"

"That in the end you will love my plan."

"And in the meantime?"

"Deal with it."

CHAPTER EIGHT

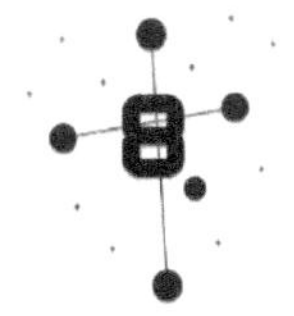

WAYWARD STATION

"The plan," Corla says, now that we've reached the end of the tunnel and are entering the park, "is to get the hell away from these crazy fucked-up people. Are you in?"

"Who *are* you?" I say.

She laughs. And God, she's pretty when she laughs. "I'm your genetically engineered princess, Crux. Duh." She stops in the middle of the grass and takes my hand. There's still that feeling hiding underneath my skin. I don't understand it, I just know every time she and I make contact I have this overwhelming urge to never let her go. "Listen." She sighs. "I don't know what they're doing. I just know you and I were brought together to make babies. Congrats, by the way. You're going to be a father."

"How do you know that? We did it once for less than five minutes."

"Trust me," she says. "I'm pregnant. They didn't drag me a hundred light years from home and set up that crazy ritual back there for nothing."

"Yeah, what was up with that? Red and black? Why am I wearing this stupid outfit?"

She looks me up and down, taking in my ceremonial uniform. "It is kinda creepy."

"Evil creepy," I say.

"Well, they are evil creepy so I guess it fits. But I'm sort of envious of you. I'd rather not have known what was coming. Your father was probably afraid you'd reject me or something. And believe me, that's not in the plan."

"OK, back up. What plan?"

She sighs, then walks over to a tree and says, "Sit. It's a long story."

I sit, and she talks, and it is a long story. But I get the main points pretty quick.

The Akeelians and Cygnians used to be one race of people. Then something catastrophic happened and they were no longer genetically compatible. So for the past however many years they've been engineering children so that one day—today, in fact—the two species could mate again and produce—wait for it—

"Stars."

"Mmm-hmmm," I say. "OK."

She makes a face at me. "I light up. Do you not find that weird?"

"You're a star?" I say. Then I laugh. I can't help it.

"That's fine," she says. "It's weird. I get it. But this light comes from somewhere. And these two races sure are trying really hard to produce children."

"Maybe they're just a bunch of sick fucks who get off on watching two teenagers get horny?"

"You think this is funny?"

"Not at all, princess. I think this is… I think… I don't fucking know what I think. But people don't turn into stars."

"OK," she says. "But maybe this thing inside me isn't people."

"Well, I'm a people. And you're a people. So it stands to reason that if we create offspring, they'll be people too."

"Maybe we're not people? Ever think of that?"

I sigh and massage the center of my forehead with two fingertips. Tired, and confused, and not ready to fight this battle, that's for sure.

"Look," Corla says, placing her hands on my shoulders. I like her touch. It makes me close my eyes and forget all this bullshit about babies, and stars, and escape plans. "You don't have to believe me. Just believe this. Something is going on. You are standing here in a creepy red and black uniform talking to a girl they set you up to breed with. That's an irrefutable fact. So if you want to forget about the baby, and the stars, and the light, cool. Let it go. But you can't just pretend that creepy clown show back there didn't happen. The only other thing you need to accept is that these people have to be stopped. Whatever is growing inside me is too powerful, that's why ALCOR helped separate the Cygnians and Akeelians thousands of years ago."

"Who?"

"ALCOR? That insane AI who runs that station that guards the gates to the Seven Sisters?"

"Go on," I say. This might actually be useful information because I sorta-kinda remember hearing about this AI from some gate-mapping class.

"ALCOR messed up the offspring of the Cygnians and Akeelians thousands of years ago and our races have been struggling to survive ever since. The Cygnians genetically engineer our daughters, then back-breed them to a previous paternal generation trying to create one girl—like me—who can actually mate with an Akeelian boy, like you."

"Oh, God. I feel sick."

"And you Akeelians… well, you guys just screw any woman who will have you, hoping that you get more boys. But—and this is the big *but*— you and your friends, like that guy you were with last night? You've been altered to match one of us. You and I were meant to be together, Crux. True soulmates, so to speak. But there's another but. Are you ready for it?"

"Hit me," I say. "I have a feeling I'll never be ready, so just give it to me straight, princess. I need to know what's happening."

"We can't ever be together. I need to get the fuck out of here. And so do you. We can't ever be together because whatever they're trying to make by putting us together—a star, a baby, a monster—doesn't matter what you call it. It just can't be born. OK? You are the one who said evil a few minutes ago and you said that because you *felt* it. But believe me, Crux. They are evil, evil people. We can't let this happen. So you are going to shoot me through the spin node where my friends will pick me up and… take care of the baby. And I'm going to send you to ALCOR Station. And we're never going to see each other again."

"Shit."

"There's more," she says.

"More? That's not enough?"

"I'm also a weapon."

I got nothing for that.

"That light inside me? It's more powerful than a sun going supernova. I am literally a bomb. They can take out entire planets with girls like me. And if they get this breeding program off the ground, the whole universe could cease to exist with the children they create."

I'm shaking my head the whole time she's talking.

"It's true," she insists. "Whether you believe me or not. Whether you help me or not. This is happening. So I need to meet up with my friends on some station on the other side of the spin node so they can… you know." She points to her stomach.

"Kill it?" I ask, horrified.

"I don't know."

"Fuck that!" I say, getting to my feet. "Fuck that! They're not… you're not… no!"

"What am I supposed to do? I'm pregnant now, like it or not. It's done. I'm not going to raise that thing."

"Thing?"

She sighs and gets to her feet. "It's not what you think, Crux. It's dangerous. These… *babies* can change everything. And not in a good way. It needs to be handled."

Handled. I just can't. I turn away from her and grab my hair, trying to force all this shit to make sense.

"We have to leave. And I have to see your friends before I go."

"Why?" I ask, turning around to face her.

"Because all of them need to leave too. And the only way I can be sure that you get all of them to ALCOR Station is to give each one of them a message to relay to him once you get there."

"And what happens if I don't get them all there?"

"Then he'll kill you. You must have them deliver my message in the correct order or he'll know you can't be trusted."

"You set me up," I say.

"They set *us* up, Crux. I'm just trying to make the best of a bad situation."

"Why do I have to go to this ALCOR Station?"

"I don't know. You just do. It's part of the plan the station people gave me. They need this AI for some reason. And he needs you." She sighs. "So. That's it."

"And I'm just supposed to trust you? Just supposed to take your word that this is all real, gather up my friends—which include two little kids, by the way—and what? Steal a ship and—" I throw up my hands. "You're insane."

"It's the only choice you have left. Believe me, if you're still here tomorrow your life becomes a living nightmare. They will sedate you and farm you for…" She looks down at my groin area. "You know. Sperm. Then they'll use you to make more babies. And if I stay, they'll be harvesting my eggs the second after I give birth. I won't live to see this baby grow up, that's for sure. So…" She sighs. "Choose then. Stay here and be a lab rat or do as I say and live to fight another day."

"And I thought I got lucky," I say.

"What?" She scowls at me.

"'Oh, Crux. You got yourself a princess for a soulmate. A beautiful silver-haired Cygnian princess. Go you.'"

She makes a face. "I'm sorry I'm not the princess you were expecting. But that's all I have going for me now. Be the unexpected."

I turn away and pace the grass in front of the tree.

"So are you in? Or not?"

"I don't really have a choice, do I?"

"Not if you want to live, you don't."

"How do you know this ALCOR will help us?"

"Let's just say… it's in his best interest to keep you alive for another twenty years."

"Just twenty, huh?" I force a smile, seeing if she'll take the bait.

She doesn't. She just shrugs. "It's going to take that long to get things ready. But you're never going to see me again. And if you do, then something has gone terribly wrong and no matter what, you need to stay away from me. Never come near me again, do you hear me? Never."

"Star-crossed." I sigh.

"What?"

"You know. Star-crossed lovers. Two ships passing in the dark. Meant to be together, but never able to be together."

She nods. "Yes. Then that's what we are. Star-crossed."

We stare into each other's eyes for a moment. Hers are still lit up with sparkles of silver. Mine, I have no idea.

"Violet," she says. "Your eyes," she clarifies. "That's how they knew you were the one. The violet inside you mixes with the silver inside me and makes… *them*. This baby, if it's ever born, will have all the bad things inside us and none of the good. They've been breeding Akeelians for your violet eyes for thousands of years and you're the first."

"And Jimmy," I say. "And Valor, and Luck, and Tray, and—oh, fuck. Serpint and Draden too. Mother of suns." I never noticed we all had the same-colored eyes. But now that she just pointed that out… it's true. I guess I just accepted violet as normal because we all looked alike. But I can't recall a single other Akeelian with my color eyes.

Corla stays silent for a few moments. Just searching my face for understanding. "Do you believe me?" she finally asks.

"I'm not sure anyone could make this up, so… I guess I do."

"Good," she says, taking my hand. "Now listen carefully. Because we only have one shot to make this work and nothing can go wrong. Understand? Nothing can go wrong."

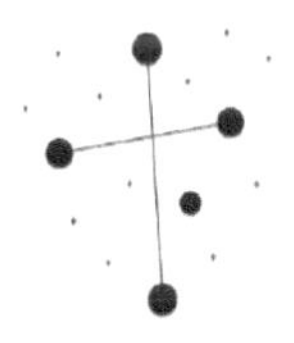

So I listened.
And I did everything right.

But something did go wrong. Because twenty years later my little brother Serpint came home to Harem Station and instead of bringing Draden with him, he brought me the one woman I was never supposed to see again.

Princess Corla locked up inside a cryopod.

CHAPTER NINE

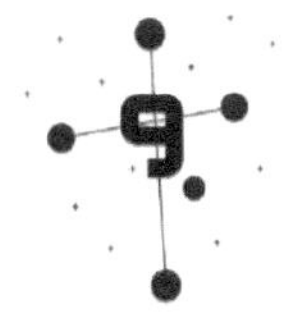

ALCOR said, "I'll help you if you help me."

Which didn't really make much sense back then. Why did I need his help again? Because yeah, station life was boring as fuck. Especially after Tray got ALCOR connected to the galactic net and we could actually see what we were missing out on. But was I in danger? Nah. If there's one thing I always felt on ALCOR's station it was safe.

But that day ALCOR told us he was going to open the station up to the unwanted and discarded—that was the first time I really felt the fear that Corla was trying to convey to me back on Wayward that night we left.

If we let people in, especially the kind of people ALCOR was talking about, then would we be safe? How could we be safe?

What is safe, anyway?

Hiding away in some forgotten part of the galaxy? Living on a station so big it can hold several million people, yet right now it only holds eight? Nine, I guess, if you include ALCOR.

I remember walking out of the pod that day ALCOR told us this. Stepping out onto the grand concourse and walking over to the edge. Leaning over, then glancing up. Hundreds of levels all empty. The silence inside. The darkness. The stillness.

This was my reality but the whole thing was an illusion.

Because outside, beyond those gates there were trillions of people, and billions of planets, and millions of systems, and so… it's not real. This quiet, still life is nothing more than an interlude.

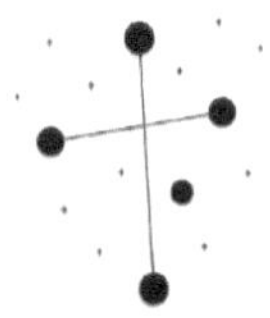

It took a couple more years after ALCOR's big speech to get everyone ready to leave the station. All of us had to become pilots, for one thing. We had to learn to fight, we had to learn to fix things. Like… everything. ALCOR made us learn how to maintain the life-support systems, and the docking bays, and the autocooks. He taught us how to build water generators, and bots, and electrical components.

And little by little he doled out his grand plan. His great mission.

We needed people. All kinds of people. But that wasn't our job. He was going to do that via some galactic advertising campaign with Tray's help.

What we specifically needed were Cygnian princesses. But when he said that all the flashing warning lights went off in my brain.

"Why?" was my first question.

And ALCOR answered, "You know why."

"To breed with them and make... *stars?*"

He was in his humanoid holographic form when this conversation took place and he shook his head no. "You only have one true mate, Crux. You already know this. They're just pretty, don't you think? Special and off limits. We're calling it Harem Station, are we not? So we need a harem. Not just any harem, one special enough that the bravest outlaws will believe our invitation is genuine and come first. Then word will get out that this is a real offer and more will come. They will come in droves to see our princesses, Crux. Millions of them will come and live here with us. And isn't that what you boys want? A home? A city filled with people, and stores, and restaurants, and entertainment? To feel part of humanity again?"

"That's it?" I asked, unable to fully buy into his sudden fatherly concern for our wants and needs. "That's the only reason?"

"For now."

I never forgot that answer. *For now.*

It made me think of time and how it's as relative as anything else in the universe.

"How long, exactly," I asked, "is *for now?*"

He didn't answer.

But he didn't have to, I guess. Corla already told me how long *for now* was.

Twenty years.

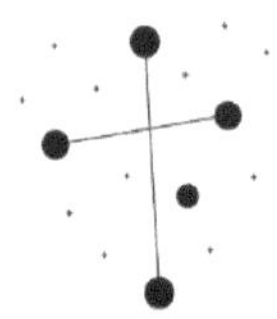

Serpint turned eighteen first, then about a hundred spins later, so did Draden. And at the time I didn't understand why ALCOR's grand plan required them to both be eighteen, but I do now.

Eighteen is the galactic age of maturity. For Akeelians, it's twenty-five, but that was just our species-specific age and since we are such a small part of the people who make up humanoid species in the galaxy, no one cared that we aged differently.

By fourteen we look like men on the outside, but inside we're still children.

By sixteen we get aggressive and competitive.

At eighteen we're downright dangerous. We call it the year of rage.

Hormones are out of whack, the urge to fight and fuck dictates pretty much every move. And believe me, that year I turned eighteen no one wanted to be around me. There were no girls to fuck. And even though Xyla offered to help me out, I said no. It wasn't right. And the only boys to fight were my little brothers. Because that's who they were by this time. Brothers.

So I just… stayed away from everyone. Just did the work ALCOR assigned me until things settled down inside my brain.

It was lonely as fuck.

Then Jimmy took his turn, then Valor, and Luck, and Tray.

It's a small miracle we didn't kill each other. But it passed over the course of half a year or so. And we had a nice two-year break between Tray and Serpint.

But Serpint was still raging pretty good when Draden took his turn and on the night of Draden's eighteenth birthday ALCOR said it was time for them to leave.

By this time we had all built at least one ship with the help of the servo bots. Who, by the way, were more than servo bots. Xyla was right. Even the ones who just mopped the floor had distinct personalities and we all had our favorites. Each of us boys had a little army of servos who followed us around like minions.

There were more than a hundred ships inside ALCOR's ring of docking bays when we arrived there, but they were all ancient. The parts were still good, and the tech was better than anything I'd ever seen or heard of. Which is a whole other story I won't go into. Because who the fuck were these people ALCOR wiped out more than twenty thousand years ago again?

Anyway, we broke the ships down and put them back together in new ways using engineering plans ALCOR stole off the net.

"One day," ALCOR told Serpint and Draden as we all stood in the airlock in front of the ship he'd assigned them, "you can tell people who you really are and where you come from. But that day is still a long way off. So…" His hologram put a finger up to his lips. "Shhhh."

"Sure," Serpint said, both annoyed with ALCOR's instructions and eager to leave. "Whatever."

ALCOR and I argued relentlessly about letting Serpint and Draden be the first to leave. But he didn't give in. And in the end, I had no choice. Because I had no real power on the station. I was just the oldest refugee and nothing more.

"Now, boys," ALCOR said. "Go forth and find me some princesses. I want *all* of them."

"Why do we need them again?" I asked.

ALCOR had picked up many of our human expressions over the years so he shot me a look that was so clearly contempt, I almost let it drop.

"I'm just getting clarification," I added, because I knew he wouldn't answer me unless I pushed him.

"To lure outlaws." He glared at me for a prolonged moment, then turned his attention back to Serpint and Draden. "The only ones you'll find will be runaways. And most of them will already belong to someone else. So…" He smiled and folded his hands at his shimmering holographic waist. "Just take them. Even if they resist, you take them. You put them in the cryopods, and you bring them straight here. I'll take care of everything once they arrive. Understand?"

"For fuck's sake," Serpint growled. "We got it, OK? Goodbye already."

And then they both put on their helmets, walked into the airlock, cycled through it, and went out into the cold, hard vacuum to enter their ship.

We watched them leave. All of us, even their loyal servos who had to stay behind.

And when they were gone this place felt a million times emptier.

CHAPTER TEN

Serpint and Draden were not even gone thirty spins when ALCOR decided it was time for Jimmy and Xyla to go on their mission.

By this time these two were inseparable friends. Jimmy was well past his year of rage and Xyla looked nothing like the sex bot who greeted us at the airlock six years prior.

I mean, yeah. She was still sexy as hell. But she took Jimmy's advice and had the medical pod remove almost all her synthetic skin and had it replaced with shining, stainless-steel armor. Her hair was still long and purple and her body was still virtual-reality perfection. But there was no doubt in your mind that Xyla the sex bot was now Xyla the warrior.

"Your mission," ALCOR told them over dinner one night, "is to round up bots."

"What kind of bots?" Xyla asked.

"I don't care," ALCOR said. "Just get as many as you can and bring them back. And tell them they don't need any credits or skills. We will teach them what they need to know. All we require is a desire to learn and be helpful."

If Xyla could snort, I'm pretty sure that's what her response would've been. "They're all gonna come then."

"Good," ALCOR said. "They are all welcome. I will have jobs for them and they will get paid. If you find any who are already in a committed contract but still want to come, buy them out." He paused for a moment, his holographic body blinking a couple times, then said, "Your credit account is full."

"How full?" Jimmy asked, raising one eyebrow.

"Unable to be emptied," ALCOR responded.

Jimmy almost giggled.

ALCOR pointed at him. "I know what you're thinking."

"What am I thinking?" Jimmy challenged back.

"You're going to buy whores. I've put restrictions on the credits."

"What the fuck? I've been here six years. I'm twenty-one years old. I need to get laid, you piece of junk!"

"Find girls who don't require payment."

"Dick," Jimmy said.

"Your future self will thank me."

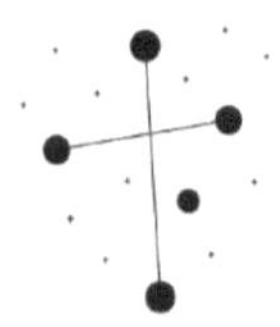

Later that night, as Xyla and Jimmy were getting ready to leave, I called ALCOR to my quarters. Tray had just installed this new quantum nanobot program in the atmosphere that acted as a comms system and I just had my comm implanted into my finger so I could access it. You just pinch the air with your fingertips and then spread them apart and a screen pops up.

I'd never seen anything like it before and it got me wondering how much we'd missed out in the real world since we arrived on the station.

But Tray said this was old tech. Stuff leftover from the station's previous inhabitants.

And once again I was thinking about who those people were. How did they have this level of tech twenty thousand years ago?

It boggles the mind. Makes you feel small and insignificant. Realizing that whole—much more technologically advanced—civilizations lived and died before your species even existed is humbling.

Anyway, I called for ALCOR and he came to me as a disembodied voice from the ceiling. Also something recently added to his repertoire of new communication skills.

"What can I do for you, Crux?"

"So this bot bullshit," I said. "What's that all about?"

"I have a soft spot for non-humanoid life forms. Go figure."

"That's it?"

"That's it."

And if he were in the room as his hologram form, I knew he'd be spreading his arms wide and smiling just as big. Because that's what he always did whenever I asked for details regarding this grand plan of his.

"I told you, Crux. I want this place to be a place of rest and respite for those who find themselves homeless."

"Right. Got that part. But something comes after that. That's the plan I'd like to hear about."

"I'm afraid my future plans are all on a need-to-know basis. And you do not yet need to know."

"I don't want to be a part of this."

"A part of what?"

"Whatever it is you're doing. I'm not going to do whatever job you have planned for me. I'd just like to make that clear now."

"Why do you think I have a plan for you?"

"Because you have a plan for everything," I said. "And Valor already told me you've been talking to him and Luck about leaving soon. So… I'm not gonna do it."

"Well, good. I do not have a plan for you, Crux. Other than…" And I swear to the sun, I could feel him shrugging. "Stay here and live out your life. Do whatever you want. Soon others will arrive. We'll have stores, and restaurants, and—"

"Entertainment places. Yeah, I've heard this speech before."

"This is your home, Crux. And I'd love it if you stayed. But no one is stopping you from leaving. There are more than a dozen flight-ready ships in the bays. If you have somewhere else to go, by all means, go."

"But that's the problem, isn't it? I don't have anywhere to go. I can't go home. Not after all this time. And I don't even have a partner. You made sure that Serpint and Draden were best friends. You made sure that Valor and Luck were best friends. And Jimmy and Xyla. And you knew Tray didn't need a best friend, because let's face it, he's barely human these days. More AI and less Tray every single spin. So that leaves me. Alone. With no one to lean on."

He was silent for so long I almost thought he left.

"I didn't make anyone be friends, Crux. You did that."

A part of me knew he was right, but he was wrong too. "I didn't make them be friends, they just… came that way."

"My point," ALCOR said. "But you're wrong, you know. You do have a best friend."

"Who?" I asked.

"Me."

CHAPTER ELEVEN

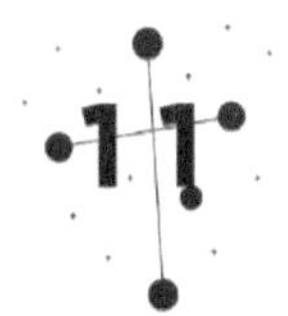

I thought about what he said to me for a long time. Months, I guess. Because that's how long it was before Valor and Luck started making their preparations to leave.

By this time I was sad. Because no one had come back. Serpint and Draden had been gone almost a full year. In less than twenty spins it would be Draden's nineteenth birthday. And I'd already missed Serpint's.

I really thought Serpint would return for that so when he didn't I just sorta went into a funk. I didn't have a job here. There was nothing to do but wander and think.

ALCOR kept me busy, but that's all it was. Just busy. I had a checklist to go through every day.

Is life working? Why, yes. It is. Because I can breathe.

Do we have nutrients in the autocook? Sure do. Because I just made breakfast.

Is there water in the reservoirs? Yup. Took a shower when I woke up.

And since Serpint, Draden, Jimmy, and Xyla were all gone now, their servos hitched their wagon to mine. So I had like thirty little bots around me at all times. It was weird, and sometimes funny, but mostly depressing because… I missed my brothers and I was desperate for them to come home and rescue me from my boredom.

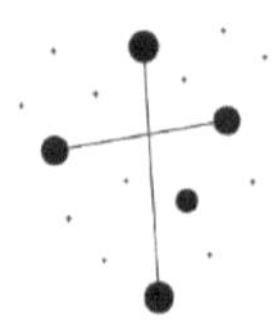

The night when Valor and Luck were leaving I really thought I was gonna lose my mind. I felt like a parent in that moment. Watching my last two kids take off and leave me behind.

Still, I managed to smile and be happy for them.

I knew I could leave. I could even go with them if I wanted. But they didn't have room for me. The ship had plenty of room, that wasn't the problem. Their brains had no room. Their hearts had no room. They were a team. And even though ALCOR said I was on his team, it didn't feel true.

"I need parts," ALCOR told them before they left. "In order to keep the station going after the people arrive I need you to go searching for parts."

So they were salvagers. And when ALCOR explained where they needed to look—far, faraway places where no one even lived—I felt a pang of jealousy. Because I knew he was sending them to the ancient sectors. The old systems with planets where whoever he killed all those eons ago used to live.

This mystery was killing me. Slowly eating away at me from the inside.

After Valor and Luck left Tray disappeared for spins at a time working on his virtual reality. Months and months went by with no word from my brothers. No new people came to the gates, asking for rest and respite.

We made stores and filled them with copies of clothes and other goods that ALCOR printed using things salvaged around the station. We made restaurants with huge commercial autocooks that could make any recipe off the net. We even built shooting galleries, and arcades, and screen houses. We had all the most recent movies from the bigger worlds. All the famous people on the screens.

But there was no one to appreciate any of it.

Just me.

I spent a lot of time thinking about Corla in those days. That one night we had together. Did she make it? Did she meet her friends on the other side? Did she have my baby? And if so, was it still alive? Was it a monster?

Was it a boy, and did he look like me? Was he growing big and strong? Did he play war games like Serpint and Draden used to?

Or was it a girl and did she look like Corla? Did she have silver hair? Did she glow when she smiled?

Star-crossed, I told her. And when I said that I felt nothing. I didn't miss the thought of not knowing her.

But in those days of boredom and waiting, I did miss her. I missed everything I never had. And I made a vow to myself. That if I ever did meet up with Corla again I'd never let her go.

I don't care what the consequences were, I'd *never* let her go.

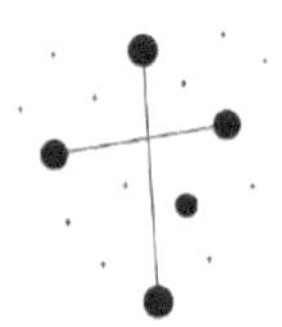

Then one day—years after my last two brothers left—there was an alarm in the station. A piercing, blaring alarm so loud and coming from every conceivable comm system, I thought my ears would explode.

I was on the lowest level. ALCOR had instructed the servos to plant new gardens down here and I was literally sitting on a bench watching things grow because he had them on some kind of nutrient accelerant.

So I looked up—all the way up. The ceiling of the ring we lived inside was so far away, the window my brothers and I stood under all those years ago when Xyla first brought us to ALCOR was just a speck of flashing red light curving around the top of the darkness.

"What the fuck is that?"

ACLOR appeared in front of me in his holographic form. Something he rarely did anymore. And he said, "We have guests."

CHAPTER TWELVE

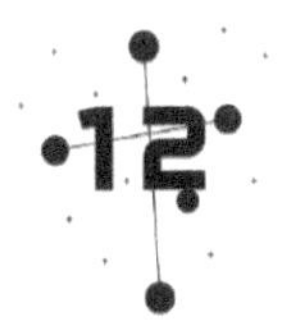

We met them on the top level under the same window where ALCOR met seven Akeelian kids almost a decade earlier.

It was one ship. But it was a special ship. A sentient ship calling herself *Booty Hunter*. And while she brought several dozen people with her, that's not the reason she came to Harem Station.

She came looking for the man called Serpint.

Who wasn't here, obviously. But hearing someone I didn't know—and yes, by this time I'd come around. All bots were people. All thinking things, no matter how simple, were people to me now—so hearing someone I didn't know say my brother's name felt like someone stabbed me in the heart.

The man called Serpint. That's what she said when she spoke to me.

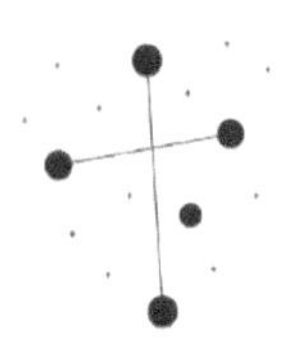

I look Serpint in the eyes now. His violet eyes that look just like mine. And I say, "You were just a kid, ya know. That's how I thought of you. Just my kid brother. And here was this powerful sentient ship showing up at my station calling you a man."

Serpint frowns, then looks out the window of the small security beacon we're sitting in. I brought him up here to tell him this story because he and Draden never really understood. They were too young to understand, so no one ever bothered to explain who we were and what we were doing. Why we left Wayward Station. Hell, he probably didn't even know it was called Wayward Station until I told him just now.

"After that everything changed. Those people in that first ship had all escaped from a prison planet. ALCOR, and Tray, and I stood there in the center of the top-level lift and he spoke to them. He told them I was the governor of Harem Station and they could stay, no payment required for the first year, as long as they worked and treated everyone with respect. All sins would be forgiven, all crimes dismissed.

"Pretty soon more people came. The levels started filling up. The restaurants opened, the shooting galleries and arcades were full, and the city… grew up."

"How long?" Serpint asks. "How long were we gone that first time?"

"Almost four years."

He shakes his head. "I didn't know, Crux. It didn't feel that long."

"Time is like that when you travel through gates," I say. "Unreliable."

He and Draden brought back four princesses when they finally returned. Four beautiful, special girls who had managed to escape Cygnia with the help of a cyborg they called Master.

"Why do you think she came looking for me?" Serpint asks.

"*Booty*? I dunno. She was never very talkative. She and ALCOR got pretty friendly and that's how you took on her galactic registration."

"She's not right, Crux. There's something wrong with her now. Ever since that attack back on Cetus Station she's been weird. Even after Tray said she was fine."

"I know, brother. That's why we're talking up here instead of down there."

Both of us look down at Harem Station, slowly spinning in the middle of deep dark space. Surrounded on two sides by two ancient gates.

"So what about her?" Serpint asks. "What do we do with her?"

We both look down at the cryopod that contains my frozen star-crossed princess and frown.

"I don't know, Serp. The only thing I do know is that I'm never letting her go again."

He nods. Sighs. "I get it. That's how I feel about Lyra."

"I knew you'd understand. And you're the only one I could talk to about this because… something is wrong inside the Pleasure Prison."

"What do you mean?"

"Tray told me once. Long time ago. That ALCOR made a copy of himself inside the prison. You know, like a backup. A *real* backup."

Serpint squints at me.

"Yes," I say, reading his mind. "Real ALCOR is living in there."

"So is *Booty*," he says.

I nod. "I know. They're up to something. I haven't told anyone else and I'm pretty sure Tray knows and is keeping it secret. So this is just between you and me. But… you know all those rumors about ALCOR being insane are true, right?"

"You think?"

"Serpint. We changed him. We did that. Us, when we came here. It changed him. That thing living inside the Pleasure Prison is Old ALCOR. Not New ALCOR. That backup was made back when we first got here. Before the Pleasure Prison was even finished. He's dangerous. And your ship, I'm sorry to say this, but *Booty Hunter* has an agenda. And it's got something to do with you."

"Me? Like… what do you mean?"

"She came asking for you, Serpint. Why? Did you ever ask her?"

"No. I don't even think I knew about that. ALCOR gave her to me and…" He shrugs. "I liked her. She's fucking dangerous, and terrifying, and so whatever, right? Got myself a new, cool ship."

"There's more to this story," I say. "Much more. And we don't have any clue where things are going now. But before we go back I have one more thing to tell you."

"OK," Serpint says.

"And it's gonna be hard to hear, so… be prepared."

"I can take it," he smiles.

I nod at him. "I know you can."

"So shoot. Tell me."

"Draden…"

"What about Draden?"

"You remember that time you two were fucking around on the bot lifts in the open space and he fell?"

"Yeah," Serpint says, furrowing his brow. "ALCOR caught him. He was fine after he came out of the medical pod."

I shake my head. "No, ALCOR missed."

"ALCOR doesn't miss," Serpint says. "He's omnipresent. And even back then we had hundreds of safety servos."

"No, he doesn't miss," I agree. "But he did that day."

"But Draden was fine. He went into medical and came out fine. I was there."

"You were there when he came out, yeah. But you were on level one hundred and seventy-three when he fell. I saw it, Serpint. I was on level twenty-six. I saw Draden fall and I looked down and there was a safety servo under him, but it didn't catch him right. He slammed into it *hard*. Draden died that day."

"No," Serpint says. "Draden died back on Cygnus Station when I stole Corla."

"No, he didn't. He died when he was thirteen and that servo did it on purpose."

"What?"

"ALCOR did it on purpose, Serpint. He let him fall onto the lift and then he popped up next to me trying to explain."

"Explain what?"

"Why Draden needed to go into a special cryopod. He killed him that day so he could use it as an excuse to get my permission to level Draden up."

Serpint just looks at me. Confused. So I decide to just spell it out.

"Draden's alive, Serpint. I know this because after what ALCOR did to him, he *can't* die."

Serpint is silent for several long minutes.

Then he says, "But... I left him behind. I left him with—"

"That's the hard part, Serp. You left him with someone I know."

"Who?"

"My son."

The next book in the series is called Big Dicker.

It's Jimmy's story and continues where Booty Hunter left off.

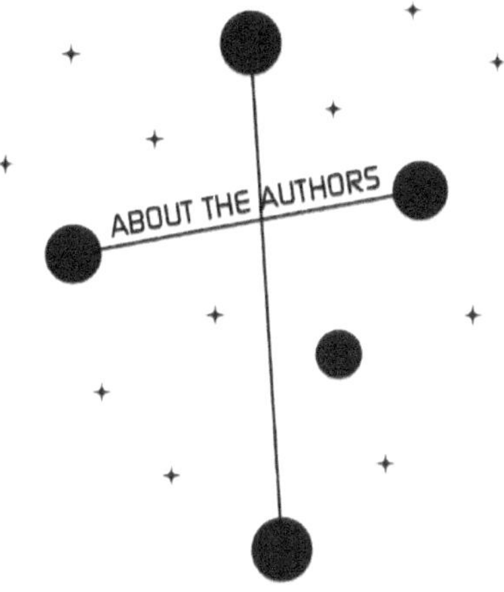

JA Huss is the New York Times Bestselling author of 321 and has been on the USA Today Bestseller's list 21 times in the past four years. She writes characters with heart, plots with twists, and perfect endings. Her books have sold millions of copies all over the world and five of her books were recently optioned by MGM Television to be made into a TV series. The audio version of her semi-autobiographical book, Eighteen, was nominated for a Voice Arts Award and an Audie Award in 2016 and 2017 respectively, her audiobook, Mr. Perfect, was nominated for a Voice Arts Award in 2017, and her audiobook, Taking Turns, was nominated for an Audie Award and a Voice Arts Award in 2018. Her book, Total Exposure, was also nominated for a RITA Award in 2019. KC Cross is her science fiction romance and paranormal romance pen name. Find out

more about both author names and their books at
www.JAHuss.com

www.ingramcontent.com/pod-product-compliance
Lightning Source LLC
Chambersburg PA
CBHW030646190726
48286CB00008B/2684